CLIFFORD THE SHEEP

SALLY SHERINGHAM

ILLUSTRATED BY PENNY IVES

· **Derrydale Books** ·
New York

Clifford was the happiest sheep in the world. He delivered newspapers and his job was to deliver the *Oakleaf Times* each morning. All the wild animals who lived near the farm looked forward to seeing him wobbling up their paths on his small red bicycle.

The animals always made sure that they had some blackcurrant tea brewing, and a pie or cake baking in the oven.

Clifford cleverly timed his visits. For example, he arrived at the Rabbits' house for tenses,

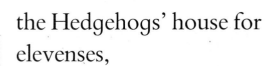

the Hedgehogs' house for elevenses,

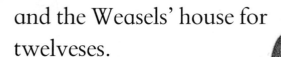

and the Weasels' house for twelveses.

Then, he always went to the Spotted Woodpecker
Inn for lunch. He loved his food and it was no
wonder that he was getting rather plump!

The animals invited Clifford in every day because he kept them up to date with what everyone was doing. He was also an excellent story-teller, so when he was a bit short of news, he made up some stories. His favourite ones were about the wicked Fox Brothers who often visited the wood.

The Fox Brothers terrified the other animals. Once they really did steal some golden-feathered chickens from Mr Grey, the badger, who was the mayor. No one had seen Mr Grey smile or laugh since that awful night.

Clifford was such a chatterbox that it took him
all day to deliver the newspapers. He never arrived
at Mr Grey's house until suppertime. Mr Grey was
getting very cross because his paper was always
delivered late.

Then, one day, Mr Grey didn't get his paper at
all! Clifford had become so plump that he had got
stuck in someone's doorway! Every animal came
to help.

'One, two, three, *pull*!' shouted Graham Rat, and out popped Clifford, like a cork. But by then it was well past everyone's bedtime, and far too late to be delivering newspapers.

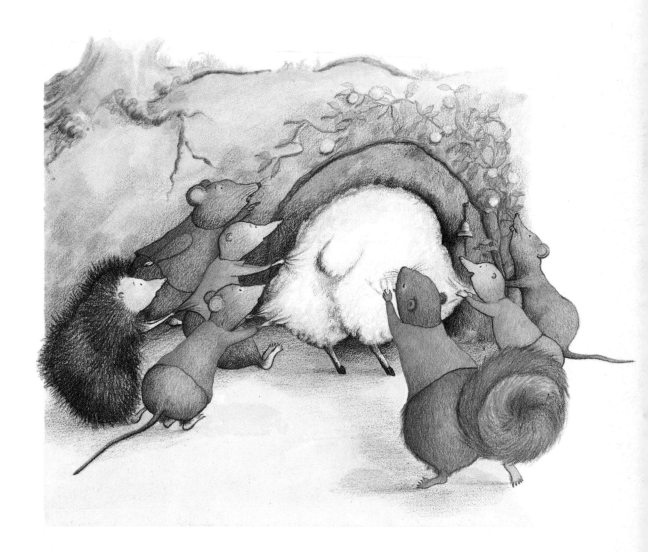

The next morning, Clifford was woken up by an angry knock on the door. It was Mr Grey. 'I have had enough of reading yesterday's news tomorrow or, in this case, reading no news at all,' he barked. 'I'm sorry, Clifford, but I shall have to give your job to somebody else. You not only talk too much, but you are clearly too fat and slow to deliver newspapers.'

So, Clifford was given a week's notice. His job was given to a stoat called Eric, who moved as fast as a roller-skater and only ever said 'Humph'.

Clifford's last day was very sad. All the animals
made an extra-special fuss of him. This meant that
he didn't arrive at Mr Grey's house till after
suppertime. He pushed the last copy of the *Oakleaf
Times* through the letter-box.

Suddenly, Clifford heard sinister laughter from inside the house. He knew that it couldn't have been Mr Grey laughing because Mr Grey never laughed. Nervously, he opened the front door and stepped inside.

There, before his eyes, were the wicked Fox Brothers. They were putting all Mr Grey's precious antiques into a sack. Then Clifford heard a muffled 'Help! Help!' coming from the grandfather clock, and sticking out of it was a grey stumpy tail. Mr Grey was shut inside the clock.

Trembling all over, Clifford crept towards the grandfather clock and unlocked it. Mr Grey slipped out and ran off to get help. Clifford was just tip-toeing after him, through the front door, when his heart sunk to his hooves.

Four sharp claws gripped his woolly shoulder!
He nearly died of fright.

'Not so fast,' said one of the Foxes, and he
slammed the door shut. Clifford was trapped!

'What a nice plump sheep,' said the other Fox.

'Er, I think I should warn you, gentlemen,'
squeaked Clifford. 'Mr Grey has gone to the
farmer for help.'

The Foxes laughed. 'Animals aren't friendly
with humans,' they said.

'Mr Grey is,' Clifford lied. 'He and the farmer play cards and drink potato brandy together every night.' Clifford chatted on and on about the farmer, and because he was such a convincing story-teller, the Foxes believed him.

Suddenly, there was a crunch on the gravel.

'That'll be the farmer now,' said Clifford.
'You'd better run or your fur will end up as orange
hearth rugs.'

The Foxes didn't wait to hear more. They ran as
fast as they could and as far as they could. In fact,
they ran so far that they were never, ever seen
again in the neighbourhood.

All the animals rushed through the door. Clifford was safe and sound! What a brave, clever sheep he was. Then Clifford told everyone how he'd fooled the wicked Fox Brothers. It was the first true story he'd ever told about them!

'Your story-telling has saved the day, Clifford,' said Mr Grey. 'I would like to apologize and to ask you to keep your job after all.' Then Mr Grey smiled for the first time since his golden-feathered chickens were stolen.

All the animals were happy, because Clifford was still going to deliver their papers and, of course, Clifford was happy too.

But what about Eric the Stoat? No one knew how he felt, because all he said was 'Humph!'

First published in 1986 by Octopus Books Limited
This 1987 edition published by Derrydale Books
Distributed by Crown Publishers, Inc.,
225 Park Avenue South,
New York,
New York 10003

© Copyright 1986 Octopus Books Limited

ISBN 0-517-65130-0

Printed in the United Kingdom